Sparrow

Sparrow

Gary Porter

RESOURCE *Publications* · Eugene, Oregon

SPARROW

Resource Publications
An Imprint of Wipf and Stock Publishers
199 W. 8th Ave., Suite 3
Eugene, OR 97401

www.wipfandstock.com

PAPERBACK ISBN: 978-1-6667-7705-5
HARDCOVER ISBN: 978-1-6667-7706-2
EBOOK ISBN: 978-1-6667-7707-9

07/13/23

For my family

His eye is on the sparrow
And I know he watches me.

—CIVILLA DURFEE MARTIN

Acknowledgements

I would like to thank everyone from Wipf and Stock Publishers who believed in me and trusted me and worked with me to bring this book into the world.

Enormous thanks to my friends and colleagues who were excited for me and who took precious time out of their busy lives to read this story and help me shape it into something far more loving and more thoughtful than I ever would have been able to do on my own, especially Paul Thompson, Aaron Gourlie, and Dr. Sally Mounts.

I owe an immense debt of gratitude to all the courageous men and women in the recovery community. This book is a tribute to their strength and humility.

Thank you to my parents who are the model of love and generosity, who never stop giving out of the depths of their hearts. They are truly a force for good in this world.

Thank you to my beautiful wife, Krista, and our son, Noah, for being the inspiration for everything I do and the source of every good thing in my life.

Chapter 1

PASTOR JUDAH GREEVES LIFTED his tired eyes from the pulpit, worn smooth under his thumbs where he'd gripped it for decades. He looked up at the dim light through the stained-glass windows and blinked. The flickering light in the rafters started him dreaming again, but he knew she wasn't really there. She was gone.

A single bead of sweat popped on his forehead and crept along the lines of his face, and he felt it on his skin like a fingernail tracing a slow path around his eye. Where did it come from? This wayward drop of water that was part of him but also somehow separate. Why did it exist at all in this world of suffering and death? What was the point of any of this calamity here on earth? It made no kind of sense. His head fell back in a sudden blind rage against God for the absurdity of it all—for the simple madness of creation. He wanted to cry out in the wilderness like the ancient Israelites in captivity. To curse God and die like Job's wife who had no name. He drew in a slow, aching breath and smelled a century of dust hanging in the air between him and God.

Creaking pews echoed off the walls as the whole congregation shifted at once in their seats. He felt their eyes burning him, and he realized he had to say something. Anything. He opened his mouth to speak, but no words came out. *Because ye speak this word, behold, I will make my words in thy mouth fire, and this people wood, and it shall devour them.* But he had no words. And no fire.

He shifted his gaze to his wife, Esther, in the front row with dull, empty eyes. There was nothing encouraging there for him.

And after all these years, there was nothing left in those eyes he could understand.

Again, the light in the rafters flickered. And he saw fireflies escape a mason jar and drift up into the stars. A single tear emerged over his eyelid and blurred the ink on his King James Bible. When he looked up, he saw *her* bright as a sunrise—flickering in the light. Her smile like light flicking off a knife blade. Her eyes shining in the twilight. Was she really there? He reached for her with bony fingers, bent and gnarled from arthritis. That white dress she wore every Sunday when she was eleven. The crimson scar on her arm when she fell in the neighbor's barn. Her laugh like a creek bubbling over the rocks.

He blinked, and she was gone. A shiver down his spine. The light flickered once more and died. He noticed the stitch in the sleeve of his suit where Esther had patched it with what used to be love. Finally starting to unravel. Head down, shoulders bowed, without a word, Pastor Greeves loped down the steps to join his wife in the front pew. His feet were heavy but made no sound like they somehow vanished with every step.

Awkwardly, the congregation of 16 stood in their Sunday best for the closing hymn, *His Eye Is On the Sparrow*—like always. A song with only voices. Their pianist passed away years ago. But they sang in harmonies learned from decades, passed down from a generation. The melody nearly forgotten like a ghost hung in the rafters. And Pastor Greeves sang the loudest.

∽

His wife, Esther, shaking, had to sit. The familiar sanctuary blurred through her tears until it almost looked like some other place. Like the blown-glass window over the kitchen sink back home when it rains—where she could see their garden sprawled out to the tree line, teeming with life. And she thought of the cereal bowl from Judah's breakfast she'd washed that morning and the sound of his spoon digging for the last few flakes. The same sound that echoed back through time when her daughter ate breakfast in that same creaking chair.

Her damp handkerchief fluttered to the floor. She glanced around the sanctuary. They were all crying. Same thing every Sunday. Same damn thing. She couldn't figure why all these old souls still came back every Sunday to torture themselves. Judah was a shade of the minister he'd once been. They could all see it. She couldn't figure why they all didn't go to The Living Waters Assembly Church across town like the rest of them. Why did anybody do anything? She had no idea.

She looked up in the rafters when she heard a flutter and glimpsed a bird dart between wood beams. Bad omen, she thought. Her mom had believed all those old myths and symbols. God rest her soul. She used to say, "A bird in the house means a death within three days." They had a bird in the house once when Esther was nine, maybe ten. Her mom chased it out with a broom, screaming at the top of her lungs and waving her broom around the kitchen like a mad woman. The hanging pots and pans clanged and rattled. Nobody died then, not that Esther could remember, but her dad came home that night after a week-long bender, and that was a kind of death for the whole family.

～

When the service ended, Judah pulled the old ladder out of the boiler room and climbed up into the rafters to change the light bulb while Esther waited in the truck. He shimmied out on a rafter and gazed down like a bird. And there she was. His daughter. A flash. Right where she'd stand when she was a girl, tying the knot he'd taught her around the new bulb for him to pull it up. He had to catch himself on a cross beam. His tears dripped between fingers. "Just the devil," he said out loud. "The devil playing tricks." He didn't know if he even believed in the devil anymore. It was just maybe a waking dream. "The king of lies," he shouted.

He cranked the window down in the truck and smelled the pines drifting in off the mountains. And the wind tossed Esther's hair. "Lot to do today," he told her. He looked down at the spider-webbed photo of his daughter when she was ten. Her wild blonde hair. That defiant, determined look in her eyes. That look he would never forget. Not for all of eternity with the hosts of heaven. The fog tore apart around their truck like a spirit disappearing into the sky.

"My heart just keeps breaking every day, Esther," he said. His hand shook on the wheel. He felt her hand slide over his, and it didn't make it any easier. Her wedding ring caught the sun and blinded him a moment. He swallowed a dry, scratchy nothing.

"There was a bird," Esther told him.

"What?"

"In the sanctuary. A bird flittin' up in the rafters." She looked over at him. "Ain't no good sign."

"The whole of creation's a bad sign, Esther."

~

This was just Judah's cross to bear, he told himself. Over and over. Just my cross to bear. God gives one to each of us. What makes us human. He pulled a 10-penny nail from between his lips and hammered it into the trellis for his blackberry bush. He wound electrical tape around the blackberry cordon to hold it in place for the winter. So much work for an old man. He'd done it all the hard way. With shovels and garden forks and hand tools. Double-digging, building raised beds, planting no till gardens. Building hoop houses by hand for the winter. He always thought he'd have a son or daughter to help him when he got old.

And Sparrow was a worker. You could never fault her for that. Skinny but tough. Worked twice as hard as any boy. And she liked the work too, didn't she? She was happy. Wasn't she?

He cracked his hammer against a rock. Sparks flew like the dawn of creation. He cracked it again and again until splinters of rock cracked off, spraying in the grass. A drop of sweat. *Is not my word like a hammer, saith the Lord; that breaketh the rock in pieces?* He cracked it again. Not knowing why. Why he was still alive, he'd never understand. A blackout of rage.

He came to in the grass, smelling the damp earth and the lavender he'd planted for pollinators. He sat up and sniffed the air. It was going to rain. He could smell it.

He thought all the anger had already spilled out of him like a broken bottle and all that was left were just worthless pieces. But he was wrong. There was still a red, hot streak of rage, creeping in through the cracks, keeping his old bones from flying apart.

He got up and stumbled over the cobblestones between garden rows. He'd carried those rocks up from the river over time in the bed of his truck. He remembered when the garden was beautiful, when it made him happy and gave him a kind of purpose. Now, it was just a burden. He couldn't keep up with it anymore. Last week, he found deer droppings in his cucumber patch and half his cucumbers gone. They had gotten in through a busted section of fence that he didn't have the time or the energy to fix. He was too old and too broke down of a man to tend this beautiful patch of earth.

∾

He crawled into bed beside Esther while the rain hit the windows. It was a peaceful rain, but his whole body ached, and sleep kept slipping away. For hours, he stared at shadows tangling on the ceiling and listened to Esther breathe. He tried to look at his hand in the dark. It was shaking. And that was God, he thought. A trembling hand you'll never see in the dark.

The phone rang. He didn't hear it. He was still fixing his eyes in the dark. It rang again. That's the devil, he thought. A ringing phone.

∾

The phone rang. Esther sat up quick in bed like rising from her grave. She slid into her slippers and ran for the phone on the dresser.

"Hello?" Her voice was dry and cracked. She cleared her throat.

"Is this Mrs. Greeves?"

"Yes. This is she," she said.

"Are you Sparrow's Mom?"

Her hand rose to her mouth. She trembled a second and felt the tears coming in her throat. "Yes," she said, but it came out a gasp. Six years. Six years waiting for this call. A call to give her hope or closure or something. She needed something. Anything but this feeling she'd had for six years.

"I'm a friend of Sparrow's."

"Judah," she hollered. A voice like a frog's croak. "Judah!" She changed her grip on the phone. "Is she ok?"

"I'm sorry, Mrs. Greeves."

"What?"

"I'm sorry. She died."

"What? What? Judah!" The phone clattered. She hit the floor in her nightgown. Her hair spilled over the hardwood.

"Hello?" Judah Greeves picked up the phone. "Who is this?"

"Mr. Greeves?"

"Yes."

"I'm sorry, sir. Sparrow's dead."

He could hear the young man swallow over the phone. "Who are you," he asked.

"I'm sorry. She's at Blessed Heart Hospital in Brier Bend, Minnesota. It was an overdose." He hung up.

The word of God is quick, and powerful, and sharper than any sword, piercing, even rending asunder the soul and spirit, and the joints and marrow.

A snake crawled up out of Judah's gut and vomited on the floor. He knelt as if in prayer. The phone started beeping. His heartbeat thumped behind his ears. How was he even still alive if his girl was dead. It was impossible.

Chapter 2

ESTHER PEEKED HER HEAD into Sparrow's old room. The door creaked open. The hinges hadn't moved in years. The room looked exactly like it did the day she left—the bed still unmade, her clothes still in piles on the floor. That weird poster for some rock band still up over her bed. The room even still smelled like Sparrow's organic shampoo they had to drive all the way into Ninevah Hills to get every couple months. Nineteen dollars a bottle! When they couldn't afford meat for Sunday night dinner and had to eat tuna fish three days a week, Judah was traipsing her off half-way to Yeden and back, spending a small fortune on soap.

Why did she still resent that so much? Why would she even think of that now of all times? The clock over the desk ticked and ticked. The radiator kicked on. The wind howled, and Esther looked over to the picture window by the bed, but it was too dark to see out.

∼

Early the next morning, when the sun was just peeking over the hills, Judah and Esther packed up the old Ford F-150. Esther wanted to say the old truck wasn't going to make it. She wanted to say something mean and hurtful, but she couldn't say anything at all. Her throat was hollow—a deep, echoing well crawling with spiders. And she was somehow trapped in the mud at the bottom, gazing up out at the stars.

With the window down, wind slapped hair in her face, but she couldn't move her hands to fix it. They were lead weights. She wanted to tell Judah to slow down, but she couldn't. And if she did, it would be a raspy, shattering howl that would cave in the earth. Sunlight spilled through the wall of pines. She had to close her eyes. And just listen to the tires against the road.

~

Judah couldn't remember when he'd realized the infinite sadness of the Old Testament. The theme of it all seemed to be the epic failure of mankind. Made him wish he'd never been born to tell you the truth. Sometimes, at night, he'd pray that the earth would just crash into the sun and burn everything to dust. But he always immediately felt guilty and prayed again to cancel that first prayer.

They drove past the church. Their church. Bethel Hollow Bible Chapel. Tiny, old, brick church falling down. Couldn't afford to do anything about it. Nobody had any money around here no more.

And he thought of Sparrow, alone, taking her last breath, staring up at a white ceiling and bright lights in some strange place with strange people gaping at her. So scared. And he wasn't there. He couldn't imagine it, couldn't fathom it. It couldn't be true. Not there to hold her. To tell her he loved her every day and that she brought beauty and love and purpose into a miserable life. Not there to pray and ask God to protect her when she goes off where he can't follow. Not happening. God wouldn't let that happen. If there was really a God, He would stop it. He would breathe life back into her. He would unwind time and bring her back. He would part the Earth like the Red Sea and keep his Sparrow from leaving.

~

Esther fell asleep, with her forehead pressed awkwardly against the car window, dreaming of Sparrow. Things she'd forgot. That damn goat. Sparrow named it Moxie and saved it from a black bear when it was just a kid and showed it more love than any of God's creatures has a right to. And that time Sparrow was asking for the key to the shed, so she could get out her Daddy's knife and play with it. She was about seven. Esther didn't want her to play with the knife, didn't like that Judah let her. So she said no, but Sparrow kept asking and whining. So she did something that would have made her daughter light up just a few years earlier. She held out her hand and slowly opened her fingers to reveal . . . an empty palm. A trick of imagination. A magic key that could unlock the whole garden. But Sparrow slapped her hand and ran away, crying her little head off.

And how could she have possibly forgotten the Sunday afternoon backyard barbeque at the Gazy's place over in Bethel Crossing and how Sparrow got drunk on whiskey the Gazy boy stole from the root cellar, and they found her in the creek, dress torn and muddy, half naked? She was twelve. How could she have let herself forget even a single moment? At the end of her dream, Sparrow was falling. Falling from nothing, through nothing, and into nothing. Just falling, hair flailing. Icy blue eyes, gaping.

～

The truck pulled in a gravel lot, rocks kicking up in the undercarriage. They pulled into a roadside diner for lunch.

They never blamed each other for how Sparrow turned out. They hardly talked about her at all after she left. It was just one of those things that happened, and there was never any clear reason why. "There wasn't a single thing you could've done to love that child any better," Liota Davis had told them one Sunday after church. "God is gonna work all this trouble out for good. You'll see," she told them.

"What now, Liota," Pastor Greeves wanted to say as he buttered his pancakes. "What now? Our little girl is dead. And God doesn't even care. What now?" But he didn't say it. He just kept on buttering his pancakes.

Suddenly, his hand shook, and he dropped the knife. "Did we screw it up," he asked his wife through a sudden gush of tears. "Did we not love her enough?"

"Judah, no. This is not our fault. You can't think like that. It's not our fault."

9

"But it is our fault. God trusted her little soul in our hands." He flashed to Sparrow sleeping in his hands. A baby no bigger than a milk jug. "She was our beautiful, little gift. And we ruined her." He buried his head in his hands. He couldn't say anything more.

Esther started to reach across the table but stopped. We can't think like that, she told herself. We just can't.

"We should've been harder on her, Esther," he continued after a moment to collect himself. "We should've locked her in her room at night and taken away her cell phone. We should've spanked her with a willow switch like my Dad done to me. Anything." His fist hit the table, weakly. A tear slipped through his beard. "Anything to keep this day from coming." His head folded down into his hands, and he was crying silently through his fingers, his shoulders slowly going up and down.

She didn't want to argue with him, so she said nothing. But he had it all wrong. He was the one that let Sparrow get away with everything. Esther always wanted to crack down on her at every turn. And he just let her run wild. They ended up sending that poor girl so many mixed messages. In those years, the three years before Sparrow ran away, they were constantly shouting—shouting at her, shouting at each other, shouting at God. Every single moment of those years was tense and dripping with fear. That's what it was. Fear. They were constantly afraid.

And looking back on it now, she thinks maybe they were too hard on that girl. Esther did actually lock her in her room many times without Judah ever knowing, and she went out the window every time. So she screwed the window shut, and that girl somehow found her way into the attic and shimmied down a drain pipe. Sparrow was tough—the most willful girl Esther had ever known. Esther should have never done any of that behind Judah's back. They should have been more of a team.

And maybe, in the end, they were actually too hard on her. Maybe every time they laid down the law on that little girl, that's what caused her to fight back. Maybe he'd been right all along. If they would've just let her go, maybe she would've eventually come back to them on her own. Now they would never know.

～

The pickup rattled down route 80. Judah listened to the tires over the road, and he could tell they were going bald just from the sound. He had winter tires stacked in the mini-barn he'd been meaning to put on for about two years. But it didn't much matter. Only place they ever drove anymore was to the church, the grocer's, the farmers' market, and back. What did it really matter anyway in the great scheme of things? We're all just specks of dirt flying around the sun on a rock.

The rolling hills had given way to long stretches of flat land, and everything looked the same. They must have crossed over into Ohio at some point. The sunset scratched red and blue across the sky like a giant bruise. A tear rolled off his chin.

"Why should I feel discouraged? Why should the shadows come?" He wasn't singing exactly, just whimpering out the words—same words each time the sun went down without his Sparrow. "I sing because I'm happy. I sing because I am free. His eye is on the Sparrow. And I know he watches . . . her."

～

Esther watched the white line roll out like a spool beside the truck. Her forehead pressed cold against the window. That damn song. She should never have let him name that girl Sparrow. Emily or Rachel or Leah. His favorite damn hymn and his only daughter. Just one in a long list of regrets rolling out forever beside her like this damn white line.

And there was a time she loved to hear him sing. When his voice felt like home. When she would knit in her rocker by the wood stove and ask him to sing for her until the fire burnt itself out. But that was a different time. A lifetime ago.

Her fingers moved over her necklace pendant, a single pearl in a white gold setting, and she thought of a happier time. A time when Judah smiled at her and bought her nice things for no reason at all. A time when she mattered to him. When she knew he thought about her whenever they were apart. When she thought about him too.

∾

Judah gripped the steering wheel like he was strangling a snake. He wasn't used to driving long, straight stretches like this. It was messing with his mind. Back home in the hills of Bethel Hollow, Pennsylvania, the sun slashed through tree limbs, and the sky folded in on itself. And the earth twisted in ways that somehow became part of you and you were winding down into the deeper parts of yourself. He didn't understand this flat, open space, like driving into a painting and getting stuck. Just all the same flat, empty road.

He wanted to pull over. And break the windshield with a tire iron. And sprint off into the woods to die under a pile of leaves like a dog. Or lay down in the road and wait for an SUV to crush him under the tires. He pictured himself turning off the road and crashing into a gas pump. He could see their pickup burst into flames, tongues of fire flashing up into the sky. He could see his photo of Sparrow dissolving slowly into smoke. And he would meet her in the Great Hereafter.

∾

He remembered when Sparrow was fourteen, she started listening to this crazy music. She would turn it way up, and the whole house would shake. The pots and pans would rattle in the kitchen. And the sound of the electric guitar would suck the air out of every room in the house. Judah and Esther couldn't even hear each other lying in the same bed.

He remembered knocking on Sparrow's door and going into her room. She was wearing ripped up blue jeans and a tight, black, tank top. He noticed a tear rolling down her cheek. He went over to her computer and turned down the music. Then, he sat down beside her on her bed.

"I love you, sweetheart," he told her. When he went to put his arm around her, she squirmed away. And he was completely lost in that moment as a parent. She had already broken his heart so many times, he was afraid to say anything or do anything that would set her off. He just didn't have it in him on that day to get yelled at. And he had the sneaking suspicion he didn't really want to know what she had gotten herself into. That hurt him more than anything—that he could be that cold toward his own daughter, but it would just hurt him too much to know. So he said simply, "Ok." And then he left. As soon as her bedroom door shut behind him, the music cranked back up to full blast. He stood in the hallway and cried.

He should have done something that day. He should have fought for her. But he didn't.

～

When his eyes started to close, Judah pulled into a motel parking lot. It was dark. He and Esther had sat in silence for the last six hours, and there was something shocking about her voice when she finally spoke.

"Here?" Her voice was ancient and crackly. But something about the sound of it sent Judah reeling back in time. To a happier place. He bought her an ice cream cone at the Tioga County Fair. What flavor was it? He couldn't remember. And he couldn't ask her. Not anymore. That wasn't something he could ask her. They walked in the mud that day and made out on the ferris wheel and listened to some terrible band play for hours. All the sights and sounds and smells of that day flooded back to him. Cow manure and funnel cakes and the wide-open green expanse of hills in every direction.

Why that day? Maybe because it was the most he'd ever heard her talk. She talked and talked that day about nothing, about everything, about how the desks at school made her feel small. About the shoes her friend wore. And something about her voice that day just caught him. And he realized he loved it. He loved her voice. He loved the softness of it, how you had to almost lean in to hear. He loved the measured pace of it, how it rolled like thread off a spool. Fast forward 30 years to a motel parking lot in a beat-up

F-150, and he wasn't sure he loved her voice anymore. It sounded old and tired.

"Can't drive anymore," he told her. "Can't keep my eyes open. You wanna drive?"

And that was that.

There was a light on in a glass booth where they had to pay. The light was harsh on his tired eyes. He had to squint. And one bulb in the corner kept flickering. And it filled him with so much rage he had to leave. He gave Esther his wallet and walked back out to the truck.

~

Esther was somehow confused by the wallet. A total mess. Receipts from 2 years ago. Punch cards from the Bethel Bakery and the Blockbuster, which shut down years earlier. Wallet-size photos of their daughter in her Sunday dress with her curls and her big, white teeth and her bright, blue eyes. How could he live with this wallet? It weighed a thousand pounds. How could he carry it around? It broke her heart. She had to sniff back a tear. She counted out ones and fives and paid the bill.

Back out in the parking lot, Judah was leaning against the truck with his foot up on the bumper like he used to when they were young. And for a moment, she saw a shadow of the man she'd married. When she got close to him, he wiped away a tear.

"Oughtta fix that damn light bulb," he told her and snatched his wallet from her hand so quick she jumped.

~

Esther woke with a gasp, her mouth sticky, her bangs glazed against her forehead. Her mind still reeling from a dream. And for a moment, the room seemed to spin before it righted itself in the dark, and she could see a needle of light poking in through the slits in the curtain. She placed her hand over her chest and felt her heart, and it scared her.

She placed her other hand on the cold, empty pillow beside her. Where did he go? She searched the dark and found the outline of her husband in a chair by the window. She thought he was looking at her, but she couldn't be sure.

"Do you remember," she started, her voice cracking. "Remember the barbecue at the Gazy's when Sparrow was twelve?"

He turned his head away and said nothing.

Esther cleared her throat. "Do you? Was it bad as it is in my memory?"

The only sound was the rattle of the radiator beside the bed. She put her head on the pillow and fell instantly back to sleep.

Judah couldn't sleep. It was eating him up inside. Voices in his head echoed. He couldn't even really place all the voices. There was his own voice that writhed with curses and screams, sounding from inside a bottle. There was Sparrow's voice—sweet and melodic like a bird flitting in the treetops one minute and then sharp and serrated the next. There was Esther's voice soft and gentle to mask her pain. There were voices from his congregation fading in and out and slipping away before he could place them all. And then there was the voice of the devil. A voice that'd been with him ever since Sparrow left. A voice like a whisper without words—just a constant, haunting murmur.

He licked his lips and blinked. He held up his fingers in shafts of light through the curtain and moved them around. And the light moved around them in shifting golds and grays. But what was the point? What was the point of such intricate, intelligent design? What was the point of this world but pain and grief and sorrow? Why would God build such a place as this?

And all the inhabitants of the earth are reputed as nothing, and He doeth according to His will in the army of Heaven.

He woke in the truck. No idea how he got there. Still dark. He squinted at the spiderwebbed photo of his daughter and stared at it until he drifted back to sleep.

They were on the road early, when the sun was still rising. They bought a box of Lucky Charms at Kroger's and ate it right out of the box with their hands. Cereal dust stuck in the scraggle of Judah's beard and in the creases of his seat. He silently reached past his wife to get a cassette tape from the glove box. Bluegrass Hymns. The sound of it whined and warbled and scratched. Esther rolled down her window to let the wind drown out the sound.

Traffic tightened up around Chicago, so Judah pulled off I-90 to take the winding back roads where he felt more at home. They pulled into a gas station to buy a map, but they didn't have any. So Judah drove off into the unknown, keeping the rising sun at his back.

Eventually, they pulled up to a line of stopped cars and waited. Judah shifted into park and stuck his head out the window to see around the parked cars. He didn't see any signs of a wreck or a construction zone.

Then he saw it. An injured buck, with broad, majestic antlers, writhed in the middle of the road, struggling to get up, but his legs and shoulders wouldn't work. Judah watched his nostrils flare and snort, his eyes widen with fear. His hooves scratched against the pavement, but he was too injured. A man and his teenage son got out of a pickup truck. They grabbed the buck by his hooves and tossed him into the weeds by the side of the road.

With a puff of diesel exhaust the pickup truck started on down the road. Judah put the car in gear and followed, but he couldn't pull his eyes away from the lonely buck, whose bright, fearful eyes caught the sun and turned to gold.

They drove a few more hours. The sun had risen directly overhead. As they pushed north, the leaves started to turn, and pops of fiery colors changed the landscape into a painting.

Judah reached into the change tray beside the steering wheel and distractedly fingered a silver dollar. And he remembered when Sparrow was about three, she got real interested in his coin collection. He had a small collection. Wasn't worth much. He especially took a shine to silver dollars. Anyway, Sparrow always wanted to play with his coins, and he never let her. Not once. He kept them locked up on a high shelf where she could never reach them. Why in God's name had he done that? What would it matter if she dropped one down a vent or lost it in the sofa cushions? She would cry and cry and climb into her toddler bed and curl up with her blanket and cry until she couldn't cry anymore. What was wrong with him? Maybe he ruined her. Maybe it was all his fault. All of it.

The sound of the driver-side tire changed suddenly against the pavement, and the old truck starting handling funny, so he pulled off the road to check. He got out of the truck, and the door slammed on its own because of the slope they were on.

There was a nail in the tire. When he knelt down, he could hear the air leaking out. Fortunately, he kept a patch kit in the bed of his truck. He pulled out his old jack and went to work.

~

Esther sat in silence as the truck tilted underneath her and her view changed from sky to grass. She could hear the long blades of crabgrass rattle and scrape in the breeze. The smell of an impending rain storm drifted in through the open window.

She heard the lug wrench clang, and it startled her out of a daze. She dragged a sprig of hair from her face and tucked it behind her ear. But she couldn't get that day out of her mind. The day Sparrow was born. Esther had been 41 years old and scared to death. It was a hard labor. She thought she was going to die. She pushed for four hours and couldn't catch her breath for a minute of it. The pain ripped through her even after the epidural. She remembered that pain perfectly. They say when the baby is born and you hold her to your chest that you forget all the pain. That wasn't true for her. She still felt it sometimes when she'd wake up out of a dream. Just for a second. A pulse of electricity that overtook her whole body right through to the bone and lit her up with little explosions of pain all at once. Her whole body would tense up so bad she couldn't breathe. And then, suddenly, the pain would let go and dissolve away.

Sparrow came premature. Esther's water broke when she was painting the baby's room and Judah was out digging in the garden. The house they lived in wasn't any more than a shack really on a patch of land carved out of the woods. There were still pine tree stumps all over the yard that Judah grew mushrooms on.

They gave Sparrow the only real bedroom in the house, and it was no bigger than a bread box. But it had a big, bright picture window. Esther was looking out that window with a paintbrush in her hand when she felt a trickle down her leg. She sat for a second in the rocking chair and took a moment to think on how her life was about to change.

Since Sparrow came so early, they couldn't take her home from the hospital right away. For more than a month, they made the hour and twenty minute drive to the hospital in Ninevah Hills every day. Judah's garden overgrew. Most of the mushrooms came and went. If it wasn't for the hoop houses he'd built that spring, they might have starved come winter, because Esther didn't have any time for canning and making her famous pickles.

Sparrow had changed their whole world around from the moment she was born. But she was pretty as a picture. Even from her first day on this earth, she had tangles of crazy blonde hair and those striking blue eyes like bursts of a firework in the night sky.

∾

Judah was driving again. The spare tire made the truck handle a little funny, but his mind adjusted quickly, and before he knew it, he was thinking on Sparrow again. She was a complete enigma to him. He had prayed so hard to understand her, but he just never could. At least not after that Sunday barbecue at the Gazy's when she was twelve. That's when it all fell apart. Before that it had been mostly pretty easy. She was a fun and happy kid. Wasn't she?

He remembered throwing a baseball with her in the yard, something they used to do almost every day when she was eleven. She was so athletic back then. He remembered the sting of the ball in his glove and the sharp crack of sound. Her throwing motion was so smooth and easy, but the ball jumped out of her hand. That same year, she was on a co-ed soccer team, and she was the best player on the field. She was fearless. She would outscrap the boys and come out of a clump of kids with the ball on her feet every single time. She was like magic on the soccer field. He remembered a snapshot of her out on the green field with the wind whistling through the grass and her wild, blonde hair flying behind her and that determined look branded on her face. And she was just as nimble as a deer in a wide, wide field.

And it all came apart so fast. How did it happen? Suddenly, she lost all interest in everything that had ever made her happy. When she was 14, he tried to get her to help him in the garden, and she screamed her lungs out at him. And then the oddest thing happened. A strange, teenage boy came romping out of the woods on a four-wheeler, and she hopped on the back with him and was gone—like she had conjured him out of nothing with some kind of spell. She came back home two days later, strung out and half naked. What happened to his beautiful little deer running majestic and free through a wide, wide field? How did his courageous little girl turn into a broken husk of a young woman?

He watched the trees pass out the truck window. They rushed by in a blur. He wondered to himself how he had become such a broken husk of an old man.

～

When they reached Minnesota, they finally found a gas station that still sold maps. It had a hand-painted sign above the door, an attached service garage, and a single, full-serve gas pump out front. Esther bought a map, two deli sandwiches, a pint of raw milk, and some homemade beef jerky.

The tall, young man behind the counter had a trucker cap pulled down over his eyes and blue coveralls with the name Joe on the chest. His hands were stained black with oil. The whole transaction happened in slow motion. When Joe handed over her change, Esther looked past him out the window and saw her husband out in the gravel lot, leaning against the truck. And her heart broke for him. He was a ruined man. He never loved nothing in the world like he loved that little girl. And she was gaga over him too.

She had tried to teach Sparrow to knit by the wood-burning stove but all that girl wanted to do was dig in the garden with Daddy or throw a baseball with Daddy. The two of them always had a secret place together where Esther just didn't belong.

And Sparrow had him coiled around her little finger. When she was about two or three, she would cry about absolutely everything. Cry real tears. But Esther knew, could feel it in her bones, they were fake cries. She was just angling to get her way. But Judah bought the whole act hook, line, and sinker. "She's crying real tears," he would always say. Her little act got him every time. But Esther had her pegged. And she resented her for it. Resented her for how easily she held Judah's attention. How easily she bent him to her will. How much he fawned over that little girl. Why did she resent her daughter so much? A tear popped on her eyelash. She wiped it away.

∼

"We're going to claim Sparrow's body," Esther mumbled to herself when they were back out on the road.

"What," Judah asked.

She blinked at him and tilted her head. She didn't remember saying anything. "What," she responded.

"Did you say something?"

"I don't think we should have her cremated, Judah," she said unexpectedly.

"What?"

When Esther's father died, he had been cremated, and he sat there up on the mantel, over the fireplace at her Mom's house, looking down at her every time she went to visit. Every time she looked at that stupid urn up on that stupid mantel she could hear her father's stupid, crackling laugh—that derisive, resentful laugh that made her feel icky. When her Mom finally passed, she threw the urn in the trash and took it out the curb on pickup day.

"I don't think we should have her cremated . . ." she repeated.

"I don't wanna talk about it, Esther," Judah shouted. "I don't wanna talk about!"

"My father was cremated . . ."

He pulled both hands off the steering wheel and stuck his fingers in his ears like a little kid. "Esther! I don't wanna hear it! Nanananaaananana!" He just babbled nonsense over everything she tried to say. Until she stopped talking.

Finally, she turned her head away from him. What a little child he was. They were gonna have to talk about it eventually. With his hands off the wheel, the truck was veering off the road. She felt the wheels slip off the edge and into the dirt. The truck jolted. Judah grabbed the wheel and jerked it back onto the road. It squealed out of control for a few seconds before he got it back in line.

Esther felt a bubble of laughter forming in the back of her throat. She couldn't name exactly what was funny, but she could feel the laughter coming. She could feel it behind her eyes. It suddenly burst out of her, loud and wet. She was laughing uncontrollably. It was coming out in bursts and gasps. Why was she laughing? There was really nothing to laugh about. But she honestly couldn't remember the last time she had laughed, and it just felt so good to let it out. She kept picturing Judah with his fingers in his ears like an upset little toddler—and the truck slowly slipping off the road. And she laughed. She had no idea if he was trying to be funny or if he was just being a big baby. And she couldn't tell which one was funnier.

Judah cast her a crosswise look and then continued on down the road to see their dead daughter. Esther's laughter finally trailed off to silence, and her whole face wilted into a sad, hard, wrinkled clump.

The rain started to fall, clattering against the roof of the truck, and streaking down the windshield.

~

It was three more hours to Brier Bend, and it got dark by the time they pulled into town. It was a small town, but to Pastor Greeves and his wife, it was a city. It had a few tall buildings and a courthouse and houses squeezed together with nothing but a few blades of grass between them.

The hospital was easy to find. It set back in a ways, but you could see it from the main road—all lit up. There was a small parking garage. They both ached getting out of the truck. They moved real slow until their muscles and joints loosened up.

Judah was so exhausted from the drive. He hadn't been that exhausted since Sparrow was a baby and cried all night long every night. She was a charmer during the day, as quiet as could be. Everybody who saw her said she was the sweetest, beautifulest baby they'd ever seen. But when the sun went down, she was a holy terror. He would hold her in his arms like a little loaf of bread and take her on a walk through the garden, so Esther could get some sleep. Sparrow's cries never seemed so intense outside. They would walk between the raised beds and the rows of double-dug beds and the small orchard. And he taught her the names of plants, and they would stare up at the stars together, and he would make up stories, and her cries would just eventually disappear into the night.

Then, he would bring her back into her room and set her down in her crib, and all hell would break loose again. He would fall to the floor and beg God for some sleep. That was the hardest year of his whole life. But looking back on it, he wouldn't trade those night walks with his daughter in his arms for anything in the whole world.

∼

They stood in the lobby of the hospital dripping wet after a run through the rain. Esther looked up at the harsh lights against the white walls and then down at the puddle under her feet. When she tried to move forward, her shoes squeaked on the floor. And she suddenly couldn't take another step. Judah slid his arm around her shaking shoulders. They would go in together when they were both ready.

Finally, after several minutes, they squeaked together down a long, bright hallway lined with framed heads of old people. Judah hit the button for the elevator, and the doors opened immediately.

Esther dry-heaved in the elevator and hunched awkwardly with her head between her knees. When the elevator stopped, Judah gently helped her up.

For more than a few minutes, they turned around in a maze. Esther felt so helplessly alone. Like there wasn't a single human left on earth, and she was doomed to wonder these twisted hallways forever with her husband.

At last, a door swung open, and they found a desk with a person sitting at a computer screen.

"We're here for Sparrow Greeves," Judah said, his voice shaking.

"Are you family?"

"Yes."

The nurse stood up. She was short with stubby arms and a kind face. Her dark hair was pulled back in a ponytail. "We've been trying to call you," she said.

"We've been driving," Judah replied. "To get here." He licked his lips and swallowed dryly. Talking had never been so exhausting.

"You don't have a cell phone?"

Judah shook his head. "Can we see her?"

"She left about three hours ago—against doctor's orders."

"What?"

"When she came in, she was unresponsive."

"What?" Judah gripped the particle board desk like he would a pulpit and leaned against it to keep from falling over. He thought maybe the nurse was still talking, but she sounded like she was underwater. There was a pen stuck in her hair. Everything around it moved like water, but the pen stayed still. "She's alive?"

The nurse stopped talking suddenly. Her eyes shifted between Judah and Esther.

"She's alive?"

The nurse looked down at a chart on the desk. She opened and closed it. "I mean, yeah. As far as we know. I mean, she was three hours ago when she left." She looked over at the clock. "Let me get the doctor for you."

She directed the Greeves to a set of low, uncomfortable-looking plastic chairs along the wall that looked like they had been put there by mistake. Judah and Esther sat awkwardly.

After the nurse's squeaking crocs turned the corner, it was quiet enough in the hallway for Judah to hear the ticking of the clock. Esther reached over and took Judah's hand in hers. Their fingers laced together with the softness of their teenage years. A softness they'd both forgotten. But neither of them really noticed it. And then it was gone.

The doctor turned the corner in a white lab coat. Her footsteps were silent, so she was standing right in front of the Greeves before they noticed her. She was young with a splash of freckles on her cheeks. She wore a misplaced smile that made one dimple pop.

"Hi," she said. "I'm Dr. Sarah." She was tallish, and she leaned down toward the seated couple with her head tilted just enough to eclipse the ceiling light and create a fluorescent halo. "Are you Mr. and Mrs. Greeves," she asked. "Sparrow's parents?"

Esther started sobbing at the mention of her daughter's name. Dr. Sarah knelt down and placed her hand on Esther's shoulder. She pulled a tissue from her pocket and handed it to her.

Judah leaned over in front of his wife, looking the doctor dead, square in the eyes. "Is our daughter alive?"

Dr. Sarah stood back up and completely blocked the light. "Sparrow came to the ER very early in the morning yesterday," she spoke quickly but clearly. "I was here actually. It was the end of my shift. She was unresponsive. Her pupils were dilated. She wasn't breathing, so we intubated. We administered two doses of naloxone. A few minutes later, her heart stopped, so we used defibrillation and were able to restore her heartbeat. After that, she stabilized. Her heart rate and breathing returned to normal."

Dr. Sarah paused. She spoke again in a softer tone. "But it was very scary. Her heart stopped for almost three minutes. And she was driven to the ER by a friend, so we don't know when she stopped breathing. She was very lucky to not have any long-term damage. We wanted to keep her here to monitor. Three hours ago, she left against our recommendation. As far as we know, she is still alive, but she needs to come back here so we can monitor her." She knelt down again, and her awkward smile returned. "Your daughter is a fighter. But she needs help."

Judah and Esther both started weeping, leaning into each other—holding each other up while teetering in their chairs. It was an ugly scene. Like two wild animals caught in a fire. The air got heavy, and their tears dripped down the walls. Dr. Sarah couldn't watch it anymore. She walked away.

Ten minutes later, Judah pulled himself off the cold, sticky, hospital floor. He reached down to help his wife up. She took his hand, and there was something different about him.

Chapter 3

"Let's go get our girl," Judah said. His voice sounded younger somehow like they had gone back in time. Life had climbed back into his eyes. And Esther felt compelled to follow him anywhere. For a moment, they simply stood together just gazing into the depths of each other's eyes. Then, they took off down the hallway, hand in hand.

They stopped first at the front desk to see if the hospital had an address or a phone number for Sparrow. They did not. So they stepped back out into the rain. They bounded up two flights in the parking garage. The doors of their truck slammed and echoed. The engine growled to life.

"Where are we going," Esther asked.

"We're gonna find her."

"But where is she?"

"She's here. She's close. This is the closest we've been to her in six years, Esther."

Rain pattered against the roof of the truck. The windshield wipers flapped. Esther peered out the window through the streaks on the glass.

"I don't know how . . ."

"We look until we find her," he said.

~

They drove around the town of Brier Bend, Minnesota for the rest of the night in the rain. Just to get a feel for the place.

"This place is so flat," Judah told his wife. "You never even have to make a left-hand turn. It's all on a grid."

He turned down alleyways and into every little nook and crawl-space he could find. Judah was trying to memorize the roads and all the shortcuts so they could cover more ground in the morning.

Finally, at 5am, they pulled into a Walmart parking lot and fell asleep before the truck engine even cooled.

Judah was up three hours later. The sun pierced through some bunny-shaped clouds. He got out of the truck and headed into the store for a jug of water and another box of Lucky Charms. We're gonna find her, he thought. She's here. Somewhere. He watched his shoes against the white floor and the way his too-long shoelaces flopped like bunny ears. And he remembered. Sparrow was maybe six. There was a family of rabbits living in the brambles out in back of the house. He and Sparrow were pulling up the brambles so they could plant berry bushes. For years, he'd been planning a small orchard in that spot. He could tell based on the plants that grew there naturally that the soil was slightly acidic, so it was the per-fect place for another little orchard. Anyway, all their clambering in the brambles had flushed out the rabbits. Six of them scurried out from the underbrush and scattered all over the yard. Sparrow chased them, running with a joy that made Judah stop working and watch. She laughed and laughed, running in that pack of rab-bits like she was one of them. He could never forget that laugh if he lived a thousand years. The sound of her laugh on that day made the sun feel warmer and the breeze cooler. He could somehow taste the sound of it on his lips.

Finally, all the rabbits turned and headed back to their warren in the brambles. Sparrow dove right in after them, and she actually caught one of the little ones by the hind legs. She came tromping out of the brambles all scratched up over her arms and legs, but she was holding that little rabbit with all the love in the world.

It was perhaps his favorite memory of her. That laugh that started somewhere deep inside and rang out like a church bell, echo-ing off the hills. He broke down crying in the cereal aisle at Walmart.

~

When Esther woke up in the truck, Judah was crunching on Lucky Charms. He had a notebook, a pencil, and a ruler, and he was drawing maps of the town.

"This really isn't a very big town," he said without stopping his work. "I'm making a schedule for us."

He had divided the town into six sections. He drew six maps. "We'll drive for an hour at each section. Then we'll take a break and grab a bite to eat. Then we'll do it all over again," he told his wife. "Each day, we'll rotate the order of our sections, so eventually, we'll get to see each area at every hour of the day. Twelve-hour days every day. This is how we find her."

Esther hadn't seen him like this since he was plotting out their property for the garden. He made drawings with a ruler just like he was now. He constantly bit his lip and tapped his pencil just like now. Raised bed here. Double-dug beds here. No till here. Berries here. And trees in the woods out back. He had walked the whole property and charted every plant in that woods that he could name. He had a plan for everything.

But she was still skeptical. "Maybe she lives outside of town."

"But she'll still come to town."

"This could take months."

"Yes," he shot back.

"But you have to preach on Sunday."

"Those old bitties'll be fine without us, Esther. Sparrow is not fine. She needs us. Our own flesh and blood."

~

The first few weeks went as expected. They stuck to the schedule during the day. They slept in the truck at night, because they had no money for a hotel. It got colder and colder every day at sunset. They shivered together in the truck. Their breath fogged up the windows. Judah bought sleeping bags for them. His cash was getting low. But he could go to the ATM and pull money from their meager retirement savings if needed. They just had to be as frugal as possible.

Esther's legs and back and hips and neck were all knotted up from sitting in the truck all day and sleeping in the truck all night. Judah could see the pain written on her eyes and in the way she walked and the way she shifted in her seat. But she never complained. And he never brought it up. He handed her a bottle of Aleve, a tube of Icy Hot, and a jug of water.

She had cleaned out the cab of the truck while he was gone, but it still smelled like old farts. He tilted his seat forward and tossed the sleeping bags in the back. And they started their rounds for the day.

Esther shifted uncomfortably as she gazed out the window, pressing her forehead against the glass. The truck rolled over a speed bump and the pavement moved under them. Judah's key-ring tapped against the steering column. Esther's knuckles ached. Her head throbbed. She wanted to go home. She wanted to sleep in her own bed under her own blankets with her own pillow. She wanted a long, hot soak in the tub. She was losing hope. This was slowly killing her. She didn't know if she could continue this madness any longer.

~

The sun crept along the sky and started to dip below the trees and buildings. Judah felt alone. There was nothing happening in his mind. There were no thoughts, no stories, no memories, no words or images. He was alone inside his lizard brain stopping at stop signs and making left-hand turns at intersections. God had left. His own spirit had left. And there was nothing. Just a vast barren emptiness.

~

"Stop the truck," Esther shrieked! "Stop the truck," she repeated under her breath. Her heart was racing. She felt a wave of something in her bones. Something Biblical . . . when the sick woman touched Jesus' robe. When the blind man could see. She got out of the truck and put her feet on the sidewalk. She didn't see her. She felt her. She felt her daughter. A leap of blood in her veins.

She spun a slow circle, scanning the scene on the street. Cars. Lampposts. Sad, little trees sticking up through holes in the sidewalk. A stone church with tall spires. A motorcycle roared by.

And there she was. Just across the street. Coming out of a convenience store. Esther took off running across the road. A Volvo stopped short in front of her, squealing its tires. That's when Sparrow turned. And their eyes locked. For a long moment. She was high. Esther saw it. She remembered those eyes. Those pinpoint pupils. Those bloodshot irises. Wide and blue, alert and shifty. Elemental, like a shimmer of stars.

It was undeniably Sparrow. Same crazy blond hair, longer now, wilder even than before. Same long, bony arms. It was her right there in the flesh like the picture in Esther's mind she'd been dreaming about for the past six years.

∼

Judah gripped the steering wheel. He could hear his teeth clenching. And then he looked up into the rearview mirror and saw her. *For now we see through a glass, darkly; but then face to face: now I know in part; but then shall I know even as also I am known.* There she was, just standing on the sidewalk. Her bright, fearful eyes caught the sun and turned to gold. Judah's breath tangled up inside his chest. He blinked. Was she real?

∼

"Sparrow," Esther called out, the word spinning and tumbling in the air. Sparrow turned and ran away. Esther chased after her, but she was in too much pain. She fell to the ground.

Judah ran by.

"Sparrow," he called.

∼

His legs felt tight as bowstrings. A searing pain shot up his spine. His lungs burned, but he kept running. He passed another old stone church. The church bell rang. He ran like a bear was chasing him. This single moment was everything. All of time. All of eternity. Every moment of his life right here in this single ragged breath. If he could just keep up enough to see where she goes.

Sparrow turned a corner up ahead. He yelled her name again, but the word ripped up his lungs. He turned the corner just in time to see her enter a red brick apartment building on the next block up. He doubled over, gasping for air for a few seconds, then took off running again. He stopped in front of the apartment building and gripped the wrought iron railing up the front steps. He looked up. It was four floors. One of the tallest buildings around except for maybe the big stone church.

He went up the front stairs. The door was locked. There was a buzzer system on the wall with about 10 or 12 different apartment numbers. He hit all the buzzers. Eventually, the door clicked open. He leapt inside to a lobby area with a cathedral ceiling. At one time, the building was probably beautiful, but now it was just run down and faded. Peeled paint. Chipped, gray tiles on the walls and floor.

Every time he blinked, he saw Sparrow. On the walls, on the stairs, on the ceiling. His heart couldn't take it. He closed his eyes and felt the tiled floor spinning under his feet. Fireflies lit up the dark and whirled up into the sky. When Sparrow was young, she used to love catching fireflies. She would sing beautiful melodies in her little voice and close the fireflies up in a mason jar. She'd set the jar by her bed and stare at the flickering lights until she fell asleep. By morning, the fireflies would all be dead. And she would cry and cry. And they would bury them in the garden and say a prayer. But then, a week later, she'd do it all over again. And every time, she would cry again over the dead fireflies. She didn't stop doing that until she was thirteen.

He opened his eyes and looked up. There was an old-timey elevator like a cage. He slid open the door and stepped in. His shoes clanked against the metal floor. He swallowed dryly. No idea what to do next. He prayed that the Lord would guide him. Give him an answer. He pulled the lever for the top floor, and he started to cry. Big, ugly tears rolling down the wrinkles in his face. The elevator pulleys squealed, and he slowly ascended. He wiped his tears with the sleeve of his coat.

When the elevator stopped, he slid the door open. Metal clanged. There was a window open to a fire escape. A cold breeze poured in. He ducked through the open window and stepped out into the sun. The hushed traffic, far below, sounded almost calming. Sunlight and shadow striped the street. He started up the rusted-out stairs toward the roof. A green garden hose snaked up the stairs beside him. He climbed a ladder and stepped over a brick half wall. A blackbird soared silently overhead and disappeared into the sun.

When he turned around, he saw a beautiful rooftop garden. Breathtaking, actually, in some way that he couldn't quite identify at first, because it wasn't exactly beautiful to look at. There were beans and squash growing out of broken rain gutters. There were old bathtubs filled with soft, black soil that grew lovely tomatoes and cucumbers. There were hoop houses made of plastic and PVC pipe. There were greenhouse tunnels and row covers that grew peppers and greens. As he walked along the crooked paths between rows, he saw a clutch of wooden raised beds with berry bushes trained on handmade trellises.

The seed is the word of God. But that on the good ground are they, which in an honest and good heart, having heard the word, keep it, and bring forth fruit with patience.

At the center of the garden, there was a huge compost pile. Beside that stood a recycling bin filled with empty bottles of Mountain Dew. And then a small blue tent. He stepped inside. There was a Coleman heater, a stained sleeping bag, some empty Yuengling bottles, and used needles. Beside the sleeping bag was a mason jar half-filled with dead fireflies. The smell inside the tent was thick. Like sweat and booze and burnt hair.

His eye caught a pile of three used condoms on the ground beside the sleeping bag, and it shook loose a memory. They had a small produce stand that he built at the end of their lane. They opened it up three days a week in the summer and early fall to sell some of what they grew to their neighbors in the hollow. When Sparrow was twelve, they let her run the little stand by herself once a week. One day, some boys from the hollow came by on their bikes. Apparently, at least according to the boys and their parents, Sparrow let each one of them kiss her for a dollar and touch her boobs (which couldn't've been much bigger than mosquito bites back then) for ten. Supposedly, this happened every week, and she was able to save up quite a bit of cash. She actually hid the cash in the stuffing of her plush pig toy that had a gash in its neck where the stuffing popped out. She hid the cash down inside there, and by the end of the summer, she had enough to buy a pair of black, combat boots. Judah shuddered to think what she might've done for money over these last six years.

He stepped out of the rooftop tent and back out into the sun, and he looked out over the garden. "The seed is the word of God." He blinked and swallowed and sat slowly down on the concrete. He felt the grittiness of it on his fingers. Cool to the touch and hard. "The seed is the word of God." A tear erupted on his face and an arc of snot. And he laid down on the roof beside a hand-built, compost bin in a town he couldn't remember the name of, and he wept.

Chapter 4

Esther and Judah slept in that rooftop tent every night, hoping for their daughter to return. Judah maintained the garden, but when the frost hit, only the plants in the hoop houses and row covers survived. Judah and Esther fell asleep each night wrapped around the Coleman heater and shivering in each other's arms.

When they were younger, they used to go tent camping almost every weekend. Judah wanted to say this was just like the old days out camping in the woods at River Bend Park or up at Shadow Lake. But this just wasn't anything like that, so he said nothing.

One morning, they woke to eight inches of snow, but they still drove their circuit around the city for twelve hours, looking for their daughter, like they did every single day.

One warmer night, Judah sat awake in the dark, listening to the gentle, breathy tones of the Coleman heater and the faraway notes of cars pulling up to the stoplight up the street.

He couldn't figure out where all the soil came from and how Sparrow got it all up on the roof. That's what was keeping him up. How did she do it? He had found two wheelbarrows stashed on the roof, but there were tons and tons of dirt in this garden. How did she get it up the fire escape? He would ask her if he ever got to speak with her again.

Between his fingers, he had a marijuana cigarette. He looked down at it and rolled it around in his hand. Under a rock at the far corner of the garden, he had found two plastic baggies. One was filled with a white powder. The other contained six rolled cigarettes. He had taken out one of the cigarettes and placed it in his pocket before returning the other contents under the rock. He had never smoked anything before. When he was a child, in the 1960s, his Uncle Jed was home from the military. He watched Uncle Jed roll a cigarette on the back porch, looking out over the valley. The smoke rolled up gently into the sky. He never forgot the sharp, burning smell of it.

He wanted to understand his daughter. He wanted to know her in a way he had always failed to. He wanted to understand why she had thrown her life away. He wanted to feel close to her. After stepping out of the tent into the cold night air, he lit the joint with a match, placed it between his lips, and took a quick puff. A cloud of smoke curled gently into the night sky and dissolved away. Oh. Oh, it burned. Not good. At all. He started to cough in spasming heaves and ended up on his knees. He didn't puke, but there was a glob of spit and snot hanging out of his mouth when he finally stopped heaving. Slowly, he stood up, puffing out quick breaths. He felt dizzy, and he slowly lowered himself back to his knees until the stars stopped spinning. "Why would she do this to herself," he whispered.

He cracked the top off a Yuengling bottle. Yuengling had always been Sparrow's drink of choice. When he held the bottle to his lips, he remembered the smell of it on her breath when she would stumble home after a night of partying. They only lived about two hours or so from the Yuengling brewery in Pottsville, so it was what everybody drank back home. He took a drink, and it took everything he had to keep from spitting it out. So gross. Like drinking cleaning fluids. It slaked down his throat, thick and slippery. He had drunk it once before years ago. It didn't taste any better this time.

He took another drag on the joint. This time a longer one. And he held the smoke in his mouth until his eyes started to burn. Then, he blew it all out through his nose and mouth. He coughed so hard, it hurt his lungs. He thought how much someone must hate themselves to subject their body to this over and over and over. Why did she hate herself? Why was her life so terrible she had to bury it like this? Why did she have to punish herself with chemicals? Then, he had a thought that maybe she wasn't trying to bury it but plant it in the ground like a seed. To grow something new.

He flashed suddenly to a memory of Sparrow when she was about eight or nine. The two of them were alone in the church. A light bulb had just burnt out in the sanctuary, and they were fixing to change it. Judah had dragged the old ladder out of the boiler room and extended it all the way up so that it leaned against a crossbeam in the rafters. The crossbeam must have been at least thirty feet up. Just then, he remembered that he had left the door of the boiler room open, and he was scared to death the pilot light would blow out. It was an irrational fear, but he felt an urgent need to go and shut it as soon as possible.

"Stay right there," he told Sparrow. "Don't move from that spot. I'll be right back."

She didn't say a word. She just blinked up at him. He ran out of the sanctuary to go shut the boiler room door. It took him a few minutes, because he felt the need to check the pilot light. It was of course still lit. When he went back into the sanctuary, Sparrow was up in the rafters with a light bulb between her teeth, twisting off the burnt-out bulb. In that moment, he remembered thinking, she's fearless. She's absolutely fearless. And he had believed that ever since. Until this very moment standing on a rooftop in Brier Bend, Minnesota. Suddenly, it dawned on him, in a flash of insight that he believed could only have come from God, that his daughter was filled with fear. Secret fear.

"She's afraid," he said out loud, and a cold, gray cloud of breath slipped from his lips. He blinked up at the stars. His fingers curled slowly into fists. He felt his unkempt fingernails scratch against the palm of his hand. How could he have missed it for so long? Why didn't he see it? She is scared to death, he thought. And he began to cry.

He wiped the tears away with the sleeve of his coat and took another drink of Yuengling. Ahhhhh gawd! Still gross.

He pulled the bottle of pills out of his coat pocket. He had found the bottle inside a broken brick in the wall. He didn't know what it was at first. There was no script or sticker on it. When

Sparrow was 15, he found a similar-looking bottle hidden in the hole of a silver maple where a branch had broken off years ago. He found it as he was tapping the tree for sap. He noticed the white cap in the darkness of the hiding spot, and he had no idea what it was at first. Maybe a mushroom cap? When he dug it out of the hole, he puzzled over it for a long moment. At first, he didn't want to believe it was Sparrow's at all. Then, he thought maybe it was birth control pills or something. Or maybe she had some secret disease she was trying to hide? He looked up from the bottle when he heard a woodpecker. And then the song of a blackbird. And he looked around at the tree limbs swaying in the breeze. And he listened to the sounds of the leaves rattling and the crickets chirping. It was a beautiful spot. He looked up at the fractured sun through the maple limbs, and he realized in a flash that his daughter got high under this tree.

On her rooftop garden, he shook out three pills into the palm of his hand. He popped them in his mouth and washed them down with Yuengling. He laid down on his back on the cement and gazed up at a swirl of stars through a wisp of a cloud. He took another drag on the joint. The smoke curled lazily up into the stars. He wondered at the sky. How the stars are pinpricks of light so far away it's like looking back in time. He watched a show on PBS once about stars. He closed his eyes and listened to the soft sounds of cars rolling by, and he waited for the drugs to kick in.

But maybe he was the crazy one. Working himself to the bone to support a family. Preaching the good news to a handful of old ladies who probably couldn't hear most of what he was saying anyway. Digging in the garden and building raised beds and hoop houses just to scrimp and save for a retirement that might never come until he's dead. Driving around in a broke down truck for 12 hours a day, chasing after a daughter that would rather kill herself with drugs than spend another night under his roof. Maybe he was the crazy one. And maybe Sparrow had this whole strange and beautiful life figured out. Maybe dodging responsibilities and living for your own pleasures night after night under the stars was the way to go. Maybe that was the real-life message of the prodigal son. That you could just do whatever the hell you want to do your whole life and God's gonna forgive you on your dying day anyway no matter what if you just ask Him.

But then what if it's the Hindu gods or the gods of Ancient Mesopotamia or some junk that he should've been praying to all along and he winds up in some hell he's never even heard of for all eternity? And maybe Sparrow ends up in some heaven he's never heard of. Shooting up heroin in her veins on into the millennia. Or maybe they'll both just be dead as a rock, decaying back into the earth. *For I know the plans I have for you, declares the Lord. Plans to prosper you and not to harm you. Plans to give you hope and a future.* And plans for you to die and rot in the earth with earthworms crawling around in your bones.

~

Esther woke out of a dream in labor pains, clutching the sleeping bag. Jolts of electricity ripped through her. Her breaths got faster and harder. Her teeth clenched and she felt the pain shoot behind her ears and break into fissures in all directions. And then it eased, slowly, like the untightening of a vice.

But even as the labor pains soothed, there was still immense pain in her back and hips and knees and fingers. She sat up and dry swallowed two more Aleve. But they weren't helping any more— just dulling the sawblades a bit as they bore into her bones. It was the pain of the cold and sleeping on cement and rumbling around in a truck for twelve hours a day with busted springs in the seat.

When she laid back down, she heard the pills rattle. She pulled the bottle from her coat pocket. She had watched Judah place the bottle in a busted brick in the wall a few days earlier. She shook out a couple into her grimy hands and swallowed. She replaced the bottle into her pocket and laid back down.

She heard Judah rustling about outside the tent. There was a dull moonglow pouring in through the tent's fabric. Somehow, the glow reminded her of her childhood bedroom. When she was young, she used to tell her parents that she couldn't sleep, because the moon was too bright, shining in her window. Her dad told her she was being an "idiot" and to stop being "retarded."

"The moon ain't that bright," he'd snicker. "And neither are you."

But the truth was, the reason she couldn't sleep was because he'd come crashing home drunk at night and yell at her Mom and beat her until he passed out. And there was Esther in the next room blinking up at the moon, shivering under her blankets.

That was when she stopped believing in God. She prayed so hard night after night for her dad to stop hurting her mom and to stop being mean to her. For him to be nice. To tell her he loved her. That he was proud of her. But it never happened. All those prayers just withered on her lips like dead bugs. They were just wasted words. So she stopped praying. Stopped believing that God even had the power to answer prayers.

But then in tenth grade, Judah came along. And he was so gentle. And so kind. And he just seemed to see her and to understand her pain without her ever having to say a single word about it. He actually asked her questions about herself, and he listened to her answers. And she wondered if maybe somehow, this was God trying to answer her prayers from years ago. But honestly, she never really bought into that. She listened to Judah preach for decades, and none of it really ever hit home for her. It all just sounded hollow. He talked about God the Father. And the Father's love. And it would bring those nights back from so long ago when she shivered under her blankets and the moon loomed down and she could hear through the walls her father's violent, screaming rage.

~

Judah's mind started to slow down. Everything slowed down. Snowflakes drifted down. His heartbeat slowed. He breathed in deep. And there was a bubble in the back of his mind like water starting to boil up from his unconscious. And the bubbles got bigger and faster, bursting over the surface. Boiling over. And there were words. Not words. Sounds that seemed like words. But not words he'd ever heard before. But he knew what it was.

And suddenly there came a sound from heaven as of a rushing mighty wind, and it filled all the house where they were sitting. And there appeared unto them cloven tongues like as of fire, and it sat upon each of them. And they were all filled with the Holy Ghost, and began to speak with other tongues, as the Spirit gave them utterance.

He was speaking in tongues. It was the Holy Spirit come upon him. He'd never spoken in tongues. Never even believed in it. Thought it was a bunch of malarkey. But the feeling of the words springing like a fountain in his mind and spilling out from his lips was undeniable. He had no idea what he was saying, but the words were unwinding years of tangled pain and regret and self-hatred. He felt his shoulders loosen. He felt his heart open up like a story-book to a fresh, new page.

He opened his eyes. The snow was still falling. The moon hung in the sky. It was the same world, but it was also different somehow in a way he couldn't quite put a finger on. He fell asleep.

~

Three days later, Judah and Esther packed up their truck and headed home. It just got too cold and there was too much snow for them to be living in a tent. And they had no money for a hotel room. So they drove through the snow on their way out of town, which looked kind of magical, actually, covered with snow. But Judah grumbled anyway about absolutely everything. About the snow piled up on the sidewalks and how slick and slushy the roadways were and how there was only one snowplow out working and it wasn't even throwing down any salt. He was ache-y and exhausted. The rapturous, Pentecostal feeling of the Holy Spirit had burnt out like a flame and left only a dying orange glow in a pile of jagged, black ash. Maybe it hadn't been real at all. Maybe he was just going crazy. Maybe it was the devil playing tricks on him. Maybe he really was just losing his mind.

But Esther felt great. She hadn't felt so good in her joints in a long time. And she knew that Judah didn't like to drive in the snow anymore, but it was gonna be fine. And of course they were leaving town without their daughter. But she was gonna be fine. Everything was just fine.

Neither of them spoke the entire ride home. It was a deep, strange, consuming silence they both got swallowed up in. The sound of the wheels on the road and the whine of the engine and the wind through a cracked window became a part of them, circling down inside each of them—like blood in their veins.

Chapter 5

IT WAS FOUR MONTHS to the day after they left Brier Bend, Minnesota. Esther's headache subsided enough for her to start washing the dishes. She ran the water in the kitchen sink. The scent of dish soap filed the edges off the rancid smell in the house. She dipped her gloved hands in the warm, soapy water. In the sink and spilling over onto the counter, there were stacks of plates, dishes, and cereal bowls. The whole house was a mess. It was a tragic scene, really.

The house reeked like rotten cabbage or dead squirrel or something. Dirty clothes strewn over the floor and hung randomly off furniture. Empty boxes of Lucky Charms piled up around the trash can. Most days, Judah and Esther just wandered around the house, bumping into things, barely speaking more than ten words a day to each other. Judah hadn't left the house since he drove to the church to leave his letter of resignation in the crack of his office door, and that was the first day they got back from Minnesota. Nobody seemed surprised by his resignation. Nobody came knocking on their door, begging him to stay. Time just kept on flowing, like a river.

Esther had joined a knitting club that met at the old Bethel Presbyterian Church basement. She'd make her famous broccoli cheese dip and head out every Thursday with a ball of yarn and her needles. Some nights, when she came home, she'd find him lying on the floor in his robe, all splayed out like a toad that got run over by a golf cart.

Esther got headaches that knocked her down for a few hours every day. Her mouth was incredibly dry, and her tongue seemed swollen. She was grinding her teeth a lot for some reason, but other than that, she felt great. As long as she kept taking her pills once or sometimes twice a day, she actually felt young again, and her joints felt smooth and fluid. She even caught herself smiling once in a while.

She dunked her gloved hands in the soapy water and gazed out the blown-glass kitchen window that overlooked their garden. Spring was popping up outside. The snow had all melted. Leaves started sprouting. But the Greeves' garden was dead and sad and withered and choked with weeds. Sunlight seemed to tiptoe around their property, leaving it constantly draped in shadow. There was a dead rabbit in the garden, shriveled and leathery with a few tufts of fur shifting in the breeze. Bones poked through the skin on the hind legs where birds had picked away at the flesh. A pair of buzzards circled overhead.

Esther noticed a small ripple out by the tree line. At first, she thought it was just the light catching a bubble in the blown glass of the kitchen window or a bubble of soap rising up out of the water. She blinked at the ghostly image through the window as it came closer to the house. She tried to swallow. Her heart thumped so hard it hurt. Blood leapt in her throat. She dropped a dish. It shattered on the floor.

"Judah!" She shrieked. "Judah!" She ran for the door. She had never moved so quickly in all her life. She was at the door in four powerful strides. "Judah!" Her breath snagged. Her heart pounded. She ran out into the mud. Sunlight stabbed her eyes. But something wasn't right. She couldn't quite figure it out, but it didn't seem real. Was she dreaming?

~

"Judah," Esther shrieked. He ignored her the first time. He was busy sniffing the air and trying to identify all the smells in the house. When she screamed his name a second time, he wondered where she got the energy. But then, he started to think about the tone of her voice. He had maybe never heard her shout anything in the decades they had been together. And never so crisp and clear.

When she yelled his name a third time, he shot up and looked out the blown-glass window over the sink.

And he saw her. She was there. It was real—the realest thing he'd ever seen. Like the first time he ever laid eyes on her at the hospital, screaming her little head off—a head full of wet, curly blond hair. This moment was the same. Sparrow's second birth.

For this my daughter was dead, and is alive again; she was lost and is found.

His bones popped and crunched as he took off running hard over the floor and out into the sunlight and the mud and the earth and sky. He felt himself laughing. He ran past Esther. He ran through the pathways in the garden and over the cobblestones.

He hit Sparrow chest first and threw his arms around her and tackled her to the ground. They tumbled together in the grass. He laughed and laughed and laughed.

"You smell like moldy cheese," Sparrow told him, her voice muffled in his robe.

Esther leapt on top of them, and the three Greeves clung in an awkward embrace on the ground for several minutes.

"I can't breathe," Sparrow said finally, and the three of them rolled apart, but they sat side-by-side in the grass for a long time together in silence. Sparrow slid a heavy backpack off her shoulders and let it topple to the ground. She moved her fingers through the tall, wavy grass and then plucked a blade out of the ground and rubbed it between her fingers like she had never seen grass before.

Her wild hair shook in the breeze. It was a duller color than Judah remembered it. And her skin was paler. She seemed exhausted. He looked over at the scar on her arm to make sure it was still there. He put his arm around her and felt the warmth of her skin on his fingers. To make sure she was real. Like doubting Thomas, he wasn't totally convinced that resurrection was possible.

"I'm sorry," Sparrow said, breaking a long silence. Tears erupted suddenly from her eyes and spilled down her face with a stream of spit. And she leaned into her father. His arms slid around her bony shoulders.

"I love you. I love you. I love you. I love you. I love you. I love you," he told her. "I love you."

"I wanna get better," she blubbered. It came out muddled and strained through her tears.

"I'm sorry too," Judah said. "I don't think I ever really saw you. I just saw the version of you that I wanted and hoped for. And I tried to put you in a bottle when you needed to fly." He sobbed. "I'm sorry."

The two of them cried together in the grass.

～

Esther wasn't feeling the emotions she had expected to feel. Sparrow seemed so far away even though she could reach out and touch her. Why wasn't she more excited at this rapturous moment that she had been waiting on for so long? Everything just felt fine. She reached out and placed her hand on the back of her daughter's t-shirt, which was drenched with sweat. She pulled her hand away and looked down at it, somehow confused by it.

"I'm gonna make you something to eat," she said. "You must be starving." And she got up and walked back to the house.

～

Sparrow wept into her father's chest. She couldn't stop the tears even if she tried. They were spilling out of her like a flood through cracks in the dam. She felt the tears, warm and dripping on her skin and eyelashes. She felt the wind in her hair, her soaked t-shirt clinging to her back, the sun on her skin. She felt dizzy with a buzz of feelings that she couldn't quite put her finger on.

She had detoxed in the woods behind the house for three nights. She had sat in the grass, leaning back against the trunk of her favorite silver maple tree, listening to the woodpecker and the hushed sound of water rushing up the trunk. And the feeling of home was better than getting high. Even when she was on her knees barfing in the dirt or squatting to crap like an animal, it still felt good somehow.

Off in the corner of her mind even in the midst of severe cramps, searing headaches, and fever dreams, there was a soft and strangely calming glow like she was doing the right thing, and she was exactly where she needed to be. Memories from her childhood rushed through her mind like an old movie. And she felt loved. This tree loved her. That woodpecker loved her. The wind, the sky, her parents all loved her. She was loved. More loved than she had ever felt before. There was something out there that loved her even in spite of all the things she had done to hurt all the people that had ever loved her. And all those things she had done over the years to get high—that was just somebody else. That wasn't her. Like she had been a ghost for six years and was just now coming back into her body.

Chapter 6

AFTER SHE ENCOUNTERED HER parents on the street in Brier Bend a few months earlier, Sparrow freaked out, and she went and got high. Once she realized her parents had found her rooftop garden, she knew she couldn't go back there, so she spent the next two nights sleeping on the back pew of the Brier Bend United Methodist church. The wooden pew creaked and it was hard, narrow, and uncomfortable, but at least it was warm.

The front door of the church had been unlocked on those first two nights, so she just walked right in, and she was gone the next morning before anyone noticed—or so she thought. On the third night, though, the door was locked, so she did the very last thing she wanted to do. She moved in with this guy she was sort of seeing, who also happened to be her drug dealer. His name was Bump. He had a pierced eyebrow and a neck tattoo of a spider. His story was that he used to be a minor league ball player, a catcher, who washed up after he tore his shoulder to shreds and could never get his swing back. He got hooked on painkillers, and his life took a hard, left turn.

He lived in a rundown, old farmhouse just outside of town, and there was this one window in his bedroom where the wind would sneak in. It was always cold in there, and he'd run three space heaters all night in the dead of winter. Whenever Sparrow got high, she saw a little man sitting out on the roof outside that window. He was a skinny, little guy with a plaid shirt and a cowboy hat. And he just stared in at her all the time. She knew he wasn't really there, but he looked as real as her hand in front of her face, and it was comforting somehow to see him. One night, she was dreaming about this little guy sitting there on the roof like he always did, looking in through the window. But suddenly, he got up and rushed into the room through the open window. She woke up startled. And there was Bump standing over her with a Louisville Slugger. She rolled quick off the bed, and the baseball bat cracked against the headboard.

She ran for the door, but he was blocking the way. He swung the bat. She ducked and felt the wind of it toss her hair. She turned and ran out the window and stepped out onto the icy roof in her bare feet. Snow was falling slowly. She heard the wind in her ears as she crept out along the shingles and reached the spot where the little guy sometimes sat. He wasn't there. She looked back to see Bump sticking his head and shoulders out to the window, shouting crazy things at her—it might've looked kind of funny if she wasn't afraid for her life.

She slipped on the ice. Turned awkwardly in the air. She saw the sky. And it was beautiful. A soft glow of blue and white. She saw the pine trees stab the clouds. She turned in the air and saw the ground. She fell two stories and hit a blanket of snow. Miraculously, she was unhurt. She jumped up and ran back inside the house, right through the front door. She leapt over the couch and grabbed her backpack. On the end table, encased in a plastic cube, Bump's prized baseball signed by Yogi Berra, caught her eye. She took it.

She heard him crashing down the stairs, so she ran out the door and was gone.

Three days later, she snuck into his garage and climbed into the back seat of his Audi A4. She didn't want to live anymore. Her life was out of control. She felt like she was on a train headed for a cliff, and there was no way to stop it. She was powerless. Her mind was too foggy to think her way out. If she could just think she might be ok, but there was a thick rolling fog in her mind like the fogs rising up from Shadow Lake back home in the fall every morning. Her belly growled with hunger. And she remembered her home back in Bethel Hollow, PA and the beautiful garden that popped with life every spring like some kind of miracle. And her parents. And the warmth of the wood-burning stove. And the view out her bedroom window. And the rolling hills and the wide-open sky. She had lost it all. It was gone.

Bump was a drummer in a metal band. She could hear the shouts and rattles of their band practice blasting out through the wood paneling in the basement. The vocals were just angry barks. The melody sang out from the guitar, clear and dark and beautiful. She had sat in on a few of their band practices before, and the lead guitar was by far the best thing about the whole band. Everything else was just a cloud of inarticulate noise. Not surprisingly, the guitarist was the only one who didn't get high during practice.

A few weeks earlier, she had asked Dan, the guitar player, to teach her how to play. She told him she wanted to play like J Mascis. He laughed and said, "I don't know who that is, but I can teach you to play like me." So she went over to his apartment, and they sat down on his couch together. He handed her a beat-up Alvarez acoustic and taught her a few chords. When he made a move to kiss her, she kicked him directly in the balls and stormed out. She threw his guitar down the steps on her way out. She heard him call after her, "Don't tell Bump!" And she didn't.

There in Bump's garage, Sparrow listened to Dan's guitar melody rise above the chaos of the rest of the band. She closed her eyes and tried to sing a harmony with it. Her voice sounded fragile and ragged, and her notes were way out of tune. She couldn't even settle into the right key. Every note she tried clashed. Eventually, she shook her head and gave up.

Her dad had taught her how to sing harmony ages ago. She was very young, like 4 or 5, when he started taking her to the church every day to sit at the piano. He would pluck out single notes and ask her to match pitches. When she mastered that, he started playing scales, and she would sing along. Then, he would play chords and have her match the root or the third or the fifth. Then, he would play single notes and ask her to sing thirds and fifths from memory. They worked at it every day. By the time she was 8, they were singing in harmony together in the garden while they worked. She remembered it being kind of magical, their voices braiding together. He would even make up tunes on the spot, and her voice would just naturally fall into all the right notes. She wasn't sure how it happened exactly, but that magic was gone.

She missed her parents desperately, but for the past six years, she had forced herself not to think about them. Every time something reminded her of them, like when she would work on her rooftop garden or if she walked past a church with the sounds of an old hymn drifting out through open windows, she would just go get high and the feeling would go away. She ended up living her entire life in a drug-addled fog, and she chose that fog every day.

When she was a kid, she remembered feeling things so deeply, especially fear. Back then, people at church used to call her fearless, but that wasn't true at all. She was wracked with fears. They were maybe just different from what most people were afraid of. And her fears came and went, but the one fear that had stuck with her through all the years was the fear of eternity. Every day when she was growing up, her parents spoke to her about the eternity in Heaven that awaited her if she would just commit her life to Christ. But the idea of eternity freaked her out and caused her to feel urgent, relentless emotions. What the hell was an eternity? It was too much. She couldn't even imagine a life without any end. It didn't matter if it was eternity in heaven or in hell, either way it was just the idea that her life would go on forever—more than anything, that's what scared the life out of her. The thought of eternity frightened her so much that she spent hours awake every night in bed, kicking at her blankets and pacing around the rug in her bedroom. In winter, she would lie on the floor at night in the warmth of her old radiator and look around her dark room with crooked slashes of moonlight on the walls, and she would think that maybe God would let her spend eternity right there in that spot. But after only a few minutes, she was crying out to God to take away her eternity.

If her father would even just say the words "eternal life" in one of his sermons, she would immediately tense up. Her heart would race and her palms would sweat, and she would cry out to God to take the pain away. Eternal life was too much life. This feeling of life was too much, too real. It was overwhelming. It couldn't possibly go on forever. There had to be an end.

Then, when she was 12, she had her first taste of alcohol at the Gazy's Sunday Barbecue, and her eternal life was over. The feeling of being scared to death just dissolved away. But when she sobered up, the heavy feelings came back just as powerful as before. By the time she got to high school, drugs and alcohol were pretty easy to come by in her hometown. They couldn't get cable tv or high-speed internet, but they could get drugs. So she made sure she was sober as little as possible. But her parents made it hard. They made her feel guilty. And sad. And angry. And afraid. Every time she saw her mom or dad's face or heard their voices, she wanted to get high. The feeling of the wanting bubbled up inside of her. It felt like spiders crawling over her skin. The only things that made the feeling go away were cracking the cap off a Yuengling bottle or rolling a joint or crushing up a pill to snort it up her nose. She had always liked the feeling right before a high more than the high itself, because she was powerful in those moments. She was hyper alert and aware of every little detail

But she wasn't afraid.

So she spent the next six years following whatever path led her to the beautiful oblivion of drugs. She wasn't a free spirit at all like some back home had said. She was just a robot acting out whatever algorithms were most likely to lead her to drugs.

So here she was sprawled out in Bump's back seat in the dark of his garage. All the drugs on Earth couldn't keep down the pain and the hurt and the fear anymore. The only solution she had left to make it all stop was death—her last drug. She popped a whole bottle of oxy in her mouth and washed it down with a full can of Yuengling. And she laid down and waited to die. To be carried away to the next chapter in her story. She wondered for a second what it would be like. Would it be a city on a cloud with pearly gates and golden streets like her Dad had always said? Would there be flames and gnashing of teeth? Would there be an infinite warehouse of drugs to kill the pain of eternity? What she was hoping for was a simple and decisive end followed by a vast, dark ocean of nothing.

She turned onto her side. The leather upholstery made a kind of farting sound. Out of the blue, she remembered her dad taking her out into the woods behind their house. He was trying to teach her the names of all the trees and the plants and the flowers and the birds. He would make her hold the leaves of different trees and feel the slight differences in texture and thickness. He would point out the subtle differences in color or shape. One day, they heard a bird song. He looked up and pointed up into a tree.

"It's a song sparrow," he told her. "Young, male sparrows learn songs from their father. And that's what attracts the females. Not just the beauty of the melody or the quality of tone but how well the young sparrow learns from the father. She wants a partner smart enough to learn the song perfectly."

Why did a stupid bird have higher standards than she did?

And why was she remembering all this now? She hadn't thought about those nature walks with her dad in years. She was shocked at the clarity of the memory given the fogginess of her mind. She could even feel the weight and the warmth of that flannel jacket she used to wear when she was outside with her Dad. It was five sizes too big. She wondered whatever happened to that flannel. That was a good feeling, being inside that flannel.

She remembered her Dad telling her that sparrows are among the smartest of all birds. And they can even begin to recognize the facial features of humans. Sparrows can also see many different colors that humans cannot see. So even though, to us, they look kind of boring and gray, to each other, they may look much bolder and more colorful.

Somehow, that thought made her feel loved like she'd never felt before. Even her name was precious. It was something to live up to. How had she never seen it that way before?

A single tear popped on her eyelash and streaked down her cheek. She was gonna die, and all her magic would be gone. All of her thoughts and feelings would vanish forever. All the knowledge and love her parents had poured into her over the years would die along with her. And she would become a blank, empty nothing. She could feel it all slipping away. Unraveling slowly and gently at first. But quickly gaining speed and growing more violent. Her light, her color, her soul was being ripped out of her. She felt lighter and lighter like she was floating up like a balloon into a violent sky, crashing with dangerous waves against a rock.

She fell into a dark, abounding sleep.

And she was a sparrow in the rafters of a church—her mom and dad's church. Her little feet pattered on a wood beam. She blinked. She curled her toes, and her talons scratched against the wood grain. And she could see so many colors it almost hurt her eyes. She swooped in the air, and the wind kissed her feathers. She felt deeply loved. She felt powerful and free. Even though everything looked so big, she didn't feel small. She lighted gently on a wood beam high above the pulpit. She looked around at the stained-glass windows and the jigsaw of angled wood beams, and she felt completely at home.

She swooped through the air again, and there was her dad at the pulpit, bending over his King James Bible. Even from this height, she could read the words so clearly. She saw the stitch in the sleeve of his suit jacket where her mom had mended it with what used to be love. She couldn't quite see his face, but she could tell he was crying. She saw the ink smearing on the page.

And there was her mom in the front pew. She looked so sad. Her Mom always looked sad, but this was a different kind of sadness somehow—a deeper sadness. Sparrow wanted to give her a hug, but she couldn't, because she was a bird. She landed gently on another crossbeam. A light flickered somewhere close by and then went dark. Suddenly, she flashed to a memory of helping her Dad replace the bulbs in the church. He would get the ladder out of the boiler room and climb up into the rafters. She would tie a knot around the bulb, and he would pull it up on a string. Looking back on it now, it didn't really seem like much help that she was offering, but her Dad made it seem like an important job.

She looked around from her perch high above the ground. Suddenly, she felt extremely hungry and irresistibly thirsty, and there was nothing to eat or drink in this church. And she felt trapped. The walls were slowly closing in. Everything had changed so fast. The church no longer felt like home. Her eyes moved around inside of her head so fast that it was all starting to blur. She swooped through the air again in search of food, but there was nothing. She flitted back and forth from beam to beam thinking there must be a bug or something somewhere. Bugs were every-where. But there was nothing. She started to panic.

Surely, there would be food outside. But she could find no way out. Her heart was racing in her little chest, and she felt so impossibly tired. She flew over to one of the stained-glass win-dows, but there was no way out. She scanned the walls for holes between the bricks that maybe she could squeeze through, but there was nothing.

From far down below, she heard her Daddy's voice, singing "His Eye is on the Sparrow." His favorite hymn. She remembered singing that song with him almost every day. They would be out in the woods picking wild blackberries and singing that song. He loved singing the tenor part. Sometimes she would sing alto and the melody would just hang out there like a ghost between them.

Now, there were others singing with him, but his voice was the loudest, and it bounded around up in the rafters—his big, boom-ing tenor. She felt a tear work its way down through her feathers. She blinked and saw a great light behind her eyelids. When she opened her eyes, it was even brighter. She felt something like love coming from the light. The light grew and grew until it was all around her. It was infinite. It was everywhere. It was everything. Her wings opened up, and she flew into the light.

She came to in the woods. She had barfed all down her shirt. Chunks of it in her hair and on her lips and chin. She sat up in the snow, shivering, teeth chattering. She grabbed a handful of snow and wiped off her mouth. She was dying of thirst, so she ate some snow, and it broke apart in her mouth.

She felt something, a presence. It felt like love. She looked up and there was a big, old owl, on an oak branch, with the biggest, roundest eyes she had ever seen, and they were staring right at her, softly. She stared up at the bird for a long time. She swallowed a clump of wet snow, but she didn't look away. She felt so much love coming from that owl. His eyes were just pouring so much love on her that it was spilling out onto the ground. Finally, the owl turned his head. His beautiful wings stretched and blocked the sun. And he was gone. "His eye is on the sparrow." She heard an echo of her Daddy's voice slowly fade away. She blinked and belched and realized she was right next to a blackberry bramble in the middle of a dense woods.

Apparently, Bump had just dragged her out to the woods and left her to die. Wasn't so surprising, really. She saw the way he treated other girls. He was mean and violent. There was something broken inside of him, but before the baseball bat incident, he had always been sweet to her.

She got up and walked into town, following the tire tracks from Bump's Audi along the winding roads. The tracks veered around the frozen lake. It was too late in the winter. The ice was thinning, and the county had come in and taken down the ice roads. But Sparrow walked right across the frozen lake on her way back to town. She could hear the water grumbling and the ice crackling deep down underneath, but it held her up, and she crossed to the other side. When she made it back to town, she pawned Bump's signed baseball and bought a bus ticket home.

The bus trip was long and boring and smelly, but she plugged in her ear buds and listened to *Mellon Collie and the Infinite Sadness* by The Smashing Pumpkins—her favorite record. And the time just slipped away. When she was fourteen, she dated this guy for about two months. He was 28 years old and listened to heavy, sad, guitar music from the 90's like Nirvana, Dinosaur Jr, My Bloody Valentine, and The Smashing Pumpkins. He worked construction and owned his own house up in Bethel Heights. She would go there after school and get high and listen to his music turned up loud enough to make dogs whimper. At first, she got into that style of music because she knew her parents would hate it, and she would listen to it in her room every night with the volume cranked up as loud as it would go. Her whole room would vibrate with the sound. But then she heard *Mellon Collie and the Infinite Sadness*, and it just spoke to her somehow. She even used to have a poster with the album art up on the wall above her bed back home. She wondered if it was still there. Her parents had probably ripped it down the first chance they got. But then again, maybe not.

She got off the bus in Pittsburgh. The snow had already melted, and it was twenty degrees warmer than it had been in Brier Bend. She spent a couple weeks in Pittsburgh sleeping under bridges. She spent one night in Heinz Field. One day, she stood at the spot where the three rivers meet, and she looked up at the houses on the hill and the trees and the buildings and the bridges . . . and she just decided it was time to go home. She only had two oxy's left. She looked down at them in the palm of her hand. They would be the last two she would ever take.

She hitchhiked home from Pittsburgh. She had to walk the last 15 miles or so from Ninevah Hills, because no one had ever heard of Bethel Hollow. She spent her very last dime on a bottle of water at the Sheetz in Ninevah. That was the Sheetz where her parents would always stop and fuel up and fill up on snacks for road trips. Her feet were throbbing when she reached Ebenezer Bridge. There it was, just before the bridge—the same old "Welcome to Bethel Hollow" sign with the bullet holes in all three o's. Why did they never replace that stupid sign?

She stopped halfway across the bridge and finished her water. She felt the sunlight on her face and the wind in her hair and the water trickling down her throat. She looked down at the Crooked Branch River, moving slow beneath the bridge. Off in the distance, up in the craggy cliffs above the river, she noticed Breakneck Point, where supposedly a teenager had died years ago jumping off and into the Crooked Branch. Sparrow had jumped off when she was thirteen. She was drunk when she did it, and she honestly didn't care at the time whether she lived or died.

She shook away the memory. She closed her eyes, and there was a voice inside her head. "As far as the East is from the West," she heard it say. "That's how far He has removed our sins from us." She remembered that the Crooked Branch flows east to west. She turned around to face west. She crossed the bridge to the other side and looked down to see the river slowly trundle west. She followed the river with her eyes as it carved its way through the hills. The river sprawled out to the horizon and merged with the sky on into forever. And she laughed. She couldn't remember the last time she had laughed.

"Almost home," she said out loud.

Detoxing in the woods behind her parents' house, Sparrow was on her hands and knees in the wet grass, retching violently into the dirt. When she was done, she gasped for breath. She felt a stab of pain twist up between her ribs, and she ejected a hard groaning sound.

Then, she felt the wind play with her hair. The tall grass tickled her fingers and her wrists. She felt the wetness of the Earth soak through her jeans. She collapsed onto her back and watched the branches of a maple tree dance together across the sky. Sunlight babbled through the fresh leaves like a stream licking against the rocks. All things she hadn't really noticed about the world in the past six years. Things about the world she had forgotten but was slowly starting to remember. It was beautiful. It was terrifying and amazing all at once. Out of the blue, she started to cry. But then she stopped just as suddenly. She took in a deep breath and held it. Then let it out real slow. Her lips slipped apart, and the breath slowly unwound from her.

She sat up against the trunk of a tree and looked down at her dirty hands. Sunlight skated over her fingers. She noticed the crisscrossing lines on the palms of her hand. They looked like roads on a map, showing where she had been, where she was going. It was a city right there in the palm of her hand, and she looked at it for a very long time. It turned to nighttime in the little world in her hand and headlights started crawling over the roads. Houses were built. And businesses and churches. A mom was driving her son to soccer practice. A little girl was having a tea party with all her stuffies in her bedroom. An old man watched tv. A pastor was writing a sermon in the light of a single lamp in his study, and he prayed a fervent prayer of eternal salvation for the whole world.

Sparrow took a breath, and the little world was gone. It blew out like a candle. But she wasn't afraid anymore. The fear that had been a passenger in her life for so long. The fear she had been running from for as long as she could remember, it was inexplicably gone. She heard a voice. It was perhaps coming from a pair of clouds tumbling together across the sky. "It's not your fear," the voice said. "It was never your fear."

∾

"I love you," her dad said again in the warm grass at the edge of the tree line. And his arms pulled her tighter.

At last, she was all cried out. She flopped onto her back and blinked up at the slow-moving clouds, tearing apart like cotton candy. And she breathed deep, feeling her rib cage rise and fall. She laughed.

"I sing, because I'm happy," her Dad sang, suddenly. "I sing because I am free."

"His eye is on the sparrow," they sang together. Her voice was ragged and thin, but she hit the harmony he had taught her all those years ago. The notes just came out of nowhere, out of some dark, cobwebbed corner of her memory—pressing aside the stone from the tomb and emerging as if no time had passed at all. As if the last six years never happened. As if she was still clean and pure. And she was so grateful for the breath in her lungs and the blood in her veins. And she felt freer in that moment than she had ever felt in her whole life. "And I know, he watches me."